D0888160

WELCOME TO
PASSPORT TO READING
A beginning reader's ticket to a brand-new world!

Every book in this program is designed to build read-along and read-alone skills, level by level, through engaging and enriching stories. As the reader turns each page, he or she will become more confident with new vocabulary, sight words, and comprehension.

These PASSPORT TO READING levels will help you choose the perfect book for every reader.

READING TOGETHER
Read short words in simple sentence structures together to begin a reader's journey.

READING OUT LOUD
Encourage developing readers to sound out words in more complex stories with simple vocabulary.

READING INDEPENDENTLY
Newly independent readers gain confidence reading more complex sentences with higher word counts.

READY TO READ MORE
Readers prepare for chapter books with fewer illustrations and longer paragraphs.

This book features sight words from the educator-supported Dolch Sight Word List. Readers will become more familiar with these commonly used vocabulary words, increasing reading speed and fluency.

For more information, please visit www.passporttoreadingbooks.com, where each reader can add stamps to a personalized passport while traveling through story after story!

Enjoy the journey!

Little, Brown and Company

Hachette Book Group
237 Park Avenue, New York, NY 10017
Visit our website at www.lb-kids.com

LB kids is an imprint of Little, Brown and Company.
The LB kids name and logo are trademarks of Hachette Book Group, Inc.

The publisher is not responsible for websites (or their content)
that are not owned by the publisher.

First Edition: October 2012

ISBN 978-0-316-21962-4

10 9 8 7 6 5 4 3

CWM

Manufactured in the United States of America

The illustrations for this book were done in ink and color pencil on Kaecolor paper. The text was set in Baskerville, and the display type is Mayfair.

Passport to Reading titles are leveled by independent reviewers applying the standards developed by Irene Fountas and Gay Su Pinnell in *Matching Books to Readers: Using Leveled Books in Guided Reading*, Heinemann, 1999.

The ^{Very} Fairy Princess

A Fairy Merry Christmas

by Julie Andrews & Emma Walton Hamilton

Illustrated by Christine Davenier

LITTLE, BROWN & COMPANY

LB kids

Hi! My name is Gerry.

I am a fairy princess!

I know because I feel it in my heart.

Fairy princesses love to solve problems.

We love to make people smile!

We sparkle all day long.

GUESS WHAT!

Christmas is in two days!

It will be the MOST sparkly day of the year.

We have to trim the tree and deck the halls.

We have to make cookies for Santa.

I sing carols to make our spirits bright.
(A fairy princess knows how to
cheer on her team!)

I have to think about the gifts I will give.

(Fairy princesses love to give gifts,

just like Santa does.)

I empty my piggy bank.

I have four quarters, three dimes, two pennies, one hair clip…and a button.

Oh dear!

This MAY not be enough.

Mommy says the best gifts are homemade.

But there is not much time!

What can I make?

Santa has a workshop and elves
to help him make his gifts.
Maybe I need a workshop!

I run to my room.

I get out my paints, pens, paper, glitter, and glue.

I make a big sign for my door.

It says, "Fairy Princess Workshop. Do not peek!"

Then I meet with my elves.

We dig through my toy box for ideas.

I find a ball, some ribbons, a sock,

a sparkly star, and a jar of shells.

What can I make with these?

My elves are not much help.

Santa makes a list of all his gifts.

Maybe I need to make a list!

But what do I put on it?

I get a pad and pencil.

I tiptoe downstairs.

Daddy is making dinner.

His apron has a big stain on it.

I make a note on my pad.

Mommy is writing Christmas cards.

Her hair keeps falling in her eyes.

I make another note on my pad.

I peek into the living room.

Stewart is playing his trumpet.

It is very squeaky and loud.

Grandma is trying to read.

I make two more notes on my pad.

I go back to my workshop.

I look at my notes and make a list.

Then I check it twice, just like Santa.

Time to get to work!

My workshop is busier than Santa's!

I work all day.

I make a gift for EVERYONE on my list.

That night I sleep in heavenly peace!

HOORAY!

It is Christmas morning!

I DASH down the stairs, laughing all the way!
I can hardly wait for everyone to open my gifts!

Daddy opens his apron first.

The stars I painted on it really hide the stain!

Mommy puts on her hair clip.

The button and ribbons I added look very pretty!

Stewart likes the sign I made for his door.

It says "Rock Studio."

(Maybe he will practice in his own room now!)

I wrote a poem for Grandma.

She reads it out loud:

"Joy to the world,

dear Grandma.

All is merry and bright!

Do you see what I see?

Santa came last night!"

And the ball in the sock

makes a PERFECT dog toy!

Everyone LOVES their gifts!
They wonder how I knew just what to
make for them.

This is my secret....

One fairy princess

is better than TEN elves

when she REALLY lets her sparkle out!